Ghosts

Of The

Upper Peninsula of Michigan

The reader should understand that we were able
to obtain some of these stories only if we
promised to obscure the actual identity of
persons and/or property. This required us to
occasionally use fictitious names. In such cases,
the names of the people and/or the places are not
to be confused with actual places or actual
persons living or dead.

PREFACE

There have been lots of folks hanging out here on our beautiful Upper Peninsula of Michigan, even after they've crossed that great divide into the land of eternity.

Some of these can seem almost as real as a living, breathing person, and sometimes they make their presence known only with a small sound or a fleeting glimpse of something that was almost there.

However they appear to us, there seems to be a number of folks here on the U.P. who haven't quite gone away, even after they've gone away.

OTHER BOOKS BY
CHRIS SHANLEY - DILLMAN

THE BLACK POND

FINDING MY LIGHT

PEARL

I would like to dedicate this book to my awesome siblings --- my big brother, Bobby and his wife, Elizabeth, and my little brother, Danny and his wife, Megan. Thank you so much for being you.

I would like to thank the following people and sources for the assistance in writing this collection of ghost legends. The list contains people who helped in a variety of ways, from those who were kind enough to just reply to my query with a "sorry; I can't help" to one fellow who sat with me for hours weaving tale after spooky tale (Mr. Johanson, you are indeed a wonderful story teller). The list also contains a few web sites and newspaper articles. Thank you all so much!

Bruce Johanson, Linda Johanson, David Dillman, Dan Shanley, Jeniece Dix, The Ontonagon Historical Society, Mary Bergerson, Gail Kurin, Susan James, Cathy Sullivan Seblonka, Christine Pesola, Dorothea Olson, Mike Edwards and his advanced sixth grade reading class at the Washington Middle School in Calumet for their Ghosts of the Keweenaw video, Karen Angeli, Patricia Dishaw, Lori Burns, Dan McCarthy, Patti of the Bay Mills Library, Henry Colony, www.keweenaw.info, www.terrypepper.com, www.forumgarden.com, www.paranormal.about.com, www.wolf.org, and "Collections of Recollections" Crystal Falls, MI 1880-1980

TABLE OF CONTENTS

THE PAULDING LIGHT

During the latter part of the 19th century, ships and trains provided the majority of the heavier hauling in the Upper Peninsula of Michigan. They deployed exports such as timber, iron ore and copper to other ports and stations around the world. Though necessary and even exciting, both forms of transportation had very high potential for danger.

One chilly spring evening in the 1890, near the small village of Paulding, a grisly old brakeman stood atop the caboose directing the engineer as the train slowly backed into the depot. The train groaned with the weight of the copper-filled cars, and the steam-powered engine puffed black smoke into the darkening night sky with her efforts. Two lanterns, one green and one red, hung on the rear of the caboose swaying gently with the movement of the train.

Unfortunately, a dead hemlock tree had fallen during the recent wind storm and lay unbeknownst across the tracks. Before the brakeman could holler out a warning, the train collided with the tree, derailing the caboose. In an explosion of chaos, the caboose fell on its side, crushing the brakeman---killing him instantly.

Legend tells that the ghost of the brakeman lingers there today. Those lucky enough to witness his presence describe two glowing lights, one red and one white (the green-glassed lantern shattered in the accident leaving a white colored light). The lights mysteriously appear out of nowhere, slowly grow in intensity, and then disappear without a trace. Many have attempted approaching the lights, yet they always appear in the distance no matter how far one travels.

One witnessed event started out when a fellow invited a group of visiting friends for a drive in his brand new SUV. The fellow, a talented mechanic named Bruce, raised an eyebrow and asked in a spooky voice if anyone had enough guts to visit the local ghost. The visitors laughed and played along, feigning fear and terror as they headed north on State Highway 45 toward the village of Paulding. They turned left at the big, brown sign onto Robbins Pond Road and drove the dirt stretch into the woods. They pulled to a stop on the railroad grade, the raised pathway where the tracks used to lie. The tracks are long since gone, but the cleared path of the old steam engine can clearly be seen cutting through the forest. Bruce parked the SUV, but left the engine running so they could listen to music and absorb the warmth blowing through the vents.

After a while, one friend pointed down the railroad grade into the growing darkness. "Look!" she said.

Off in the distance they saw two lights, one red and one white. The lights grew brighter and appeared to be coming closer. And closer. The group fidgeted nervously in their seats, yet at the same time excitement tingled at the base of their scalps.

The lights blazed even closer still, and seemed to be coming straight down the railroad grade directly toward them! That was enough excitement for one evening.

"Let's leave," the woman's voice shook.

"I think that's a very good idea," Bruce mumbled as he jerked the gear into reverse.

But the new SUV choked off dead.

"What the—" Bruce quickly turned the key to restart the vehicle, but to no avail.

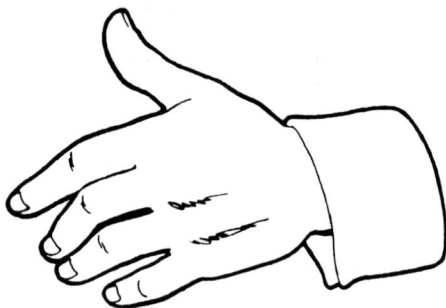

The lights bore down on the group as they stared transfixed, frozen in horror. Bruce threw his hands up just as the lights moved *through* their SUV and then disappeared.

The SUV's engine roared back to life, the music blared through the speakers, warm air burst through the vents, all without

Bruce turning the ignition key again. Bruce threw the gear into reverse and the tires spun in the gravel as they sped away without a word. Bruce drove straight to his next-door-neighbor's home, who happened to be a preacher. Sitting in his living room, they retold their spooky experience with pounding pulses. This recount has been passed on from that preacher's own lips, and everyone knows that a preacher would never lie.

BURIED BONES

The village of Ontonagon lies along the beautiful shores of Lake Superior in the western half of the Upper Peninsula. Charles LeMoine and his family lived in Ontonagon in the early 1900's. They owned a plot of land in town that once belonged to Mrs. Amanda Paul, the widow of Ontonagon's founder. And the people who lived there before her? Well, they prefer to remain anonymous and untouched...and they still reside there today.

Charles LeMoine's family knew as well as anyone, that the February winds coming in off of Lake Superior blew harsh and cold indeed. Winter snows piled up three to four feet deep and temperatures hovered below zero.

They decided that their tar-papered shack needed some vast reconstruction improvements to keep themselves warm through the long winters. They arranged for two smaller houses to be hauled to their land and compiled around the existing shack, creating one larger, cozier home for the family. Construction proceeded as planned, and all seemed fine; the family soon moved into their enhanced home.

In the summer of 1927, Charles decided that their home needed a proper foundation built beneath it. Workers jacked the house up on supports to provide access beneath the house, and then they began shoveling out the dirt below to make room for the foundation. Mr. LeMoine's family remained living in the jacked-up house while the work continued on below them.

Before too long, the workers unearthed an extraordinary find --- two woven baskets filled with human bones! A third basket contained chipped earthen pots, arrow heads, sacks of dried wild rice, and a necklace made from whitetail deer teeth and ruffed

grouse feathers. Obviously, the unearthed graves had Native American heritage. An excited Mr. LeMoine quickly called out for his neighbors and passersby to come see the discovery. A group of curious villagers crowded beneath the house to view the graves, but just then the house began to shake and tremble, to groan and grind! The villagers quickly fled the area, fearing for their lives! The quaking eventually stilled, but disarray had hit inside the house. The family found furniture topple over, pots and pans knocked off hooks, windows cracked, picture frames broken, clothes strewn about, and stove soot coating the kitchen floor. But, as the strange and unexplainable shaking seemed to have stopped, the family put the incident behind them. They set about straightening things up before retiring to bed.

The next morning, it occurred to Mr. LeMoine that a local museum or university might be interested in the ancient bones and artifacts. So he sat down and wrote a few letters of inquiry while the workers continued their digging on another part of the foundation project. Later that day, a strange odor started oozing throughout the house. Described as a mixture of decaying human flesh, old wood smoke, and the rotting pit of an outhouse, the odor caused eyes to water, stomachs to heave and nose membranes to burn. The workers quickly finished their digging for the day and left the area. Charles and his family struggled through the afternoon by tying bandanas around their noses and mouths, and by burning peppermint oil to cover the odor. Though it didn't eradicate the stench by any means, their methods did help, a bit.

Day three dawned with the horrid smell finally dispersed, but now the family discovered personal items missing. Mrs. LeMoine's silver hairbrush, Mr. LeMoine's pocket watch, a string of pearls passed down from a grandmother, a child's left shoe, a pot of potatoes waiting to be cooked, and a toy train engine all missing without a trace. Yet the family had been in the house the entire time; no thief could have entered without notice. Mr. LeMoine scratched his head in wonder. Beneath the house, all was quiet; work on the foundation had halted until a response came from the museums and universities.

Day four brought about yet another unexplainable event. The family awoke to find the walls coated in a green, mossy slime. It didn't appear to cause any damage, yet the family toiled for hours scrubbing the walls to remove the sticky goo.

Mr. LeMoine and his family awoke on day five to itchy, irritated rashes on their arms and legs. As the morning passed into afternoon, the red rashes began to burn painfully. They attempted to soothe the inflammations with creams and lotions, but nothing seemed to help. By early evening, the rashes had swelled into

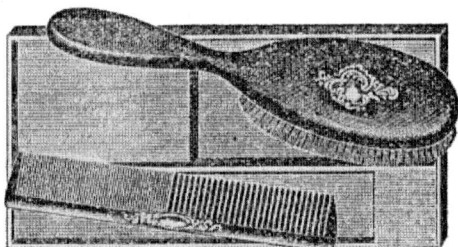

hives, pulsing and pounding with pain. While wreathing in agony, Mr. LeMoine finally grasped the concept that the strange occurrences had begun when they'd unearthed the graves. He had an idea.

Charles LeMoine climbed under the jacked-up house with a shovel. He personally heaved shovelful after shovelful of dirt back onto the bone-filled baskets. He recalled the work crew, and they soon had the cement foundation poured and curing. The rashes quietly faded. The graves now rest in peace beneath the foundation, and the LeMoine family never again suffered anything strange or troublesome in their house.

SUSPENDED LOVE

June and Peter met in 1964 at Camp Happy Hemlock where they both worked as counselors. Over the summer, in between chasing rowdy kids, bandaging cuts and scrapes and spinning spooky tales around the campfire, the young couple fell in love.

They seized every spare moment they could to spend together. Moonlit walks strolling hand-in-hand, stolen kisses shared behind the mess hall, and long, in-depth conversations filled with both laughter and tears bonded the two soul mates together forever. Only one major problem stood directly in the path for June and Peter --- June lived in St. Ignace located at the east end of the U.P., and Peter was a troll.

Not a real troll, of course. Actually, Peter stood six feet tall with curling blond hair and sky-blue eyes. In this case, a troll refers to the somewhat derogatory term for those living in the lower part of Michigan.

See, the Mackinac Bridge connects Mackinaw City in the lower part of Michigan to St. Ignace in the U.P. Folks in the lower part of Michigan live beneath the bridge, hence the nickname of trolls.

When summer came to a close and Camp Happy Hemlock's session ended, June would return to St. Ignace and Peter to his home. Both feared they would never see each other again. As the closing date approached, they desperately discussed possible solutions to no avail. But on the last day, Peter came up with the perfect plan --- they'd get married. Both had turned

eighteen over the summer, and both had finished high school, so it seemed the most logical next step. Unfortunately, both sets of parents absolutely forbade it. Peter had won a baseball scholarship to Michigan State University, and June had a year of study abroad planned in Europe. The parents feared that if the two got married, neither would fulfill their educational goals. The parents did consent that if after their schooling they still wanted to marry, then the families would proceed with a wedding.

Neither Peter nor June liked their parents' ruling. It would take forever to finish school! So they made their own plans, secret plans. They vowed that no one would keep them apart.

One week before the start of classes, June slipped out of her parents' house under the cover of darkness. She carried one suitcase and slung a backpack over her shoulders. Even after two blocks, her heart continued to pound with fear of being discovered, plus the muscles in her arms began to ache and protest. But she trudged on without complaint. She only had to walk a bit farther, and then she would fall into Peter's arms again, this time forever. He, too, snuck out of his parents' house, and would be at that very moment driving north towards the Mackinac Bridge where they would reunite and then run off to marry.

They weather had taken a turn for autumn with falling temperatures and chilling rainfalls that soaked right into one's bones. The crisp air battled with the lake's still lingering warm waters creating a misty fog that embraced the massive bridge. The thick fog along with the drenching rain and impenetrable darkness made the already imposing night a bit more daunting. But June squared her shoulders, took a deep breath and continued on to their prearranged meeting spot at the north end of the bridge.

But Peter failed to show. After waiting an hour in the cold and damp, June decided to keep walking. At least she'd get her blood moving and get warmer, plus she'd be all the closer when Peter did arrive. And of that she had no doubt;

Peter *was* coming. So she stepped onto the near empty bridge. June peered into the distance for the other side, but only a black swirling mist met her eyes. An uneasy feeling crept into her heart, but she shook it off; she just couldn't sit still any longer.

Halfway across, June came to the conclusion that walking the Mackinac Bridge hadn't been the best of ideas. The seemingly

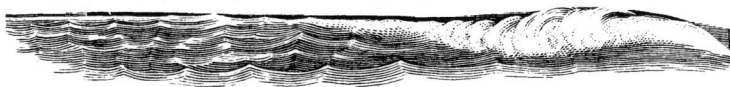

secure concrete and steel structure swayed in the galling winds while wild waves pounded and splashed up from the darkness below. And while the traffic did flow sparsely across the bridge, poor visibility had almost caused her to get run over twice already. The bridge hadn't been intended for pedestrian crossings. But by this time, retracing her steps would prove the same distance as continuing forward, she maintained her direction south across the bridge. Surely she'd meet up with Peter soon.

Meanwhile, Peter pressed down on the gas pedal to make up lost time. He'd had a flat tire, tonight of all nights, and to make matters worse, his spare had been flat as well. Running almost two hours late, he desperately hoped June hadn't given up on him. Just the thought that June might be upset, worried or be feeling abandoned forced his foot down

harder on the accelerator. He knew he drove too fast and a bit recklessly, especially for the night's low visibility conditions, but he couldn't help it; he was late for his future

He breathed a bit easier as he pulled onto the south entrance of the bridge. Not long now until he could hold June to his heart once again. But then a large gust of wind hit him broadside just as the wheels touched a patch of icy pavement, swinging the car into a tail spin. Peter desperately clutched at the wheel to regain control, not even seeing the terrified pedestrian in front of him. The car tore through the barriers, plummeting Peter and June to their deaths.

Now when the nights are starless and the misty fog rolls in over the water, June and Peter's ghostly images can be seen walking hand in hand across the Mackinac Bridge, at last together forever.

LATE FOR THE PARTY

Bright red maple and golden yellow aspen leaves danced in the crisp autumn breeze as Ben and Josh drove down the dirt road leading to their secluded cabin. Every year the brothers traveled to the Upper Peninsula for a two week reunion with their pals Robby and Stewart. The rustic cabin sat on a parcel of land nestled up

next to the vast acreage of the Ottawa National Forest. The long-time friends spent their much anticipated vacation hiking beneath the colorful fall foliage, fishing on lakes shared with the migrating Canada geese, canoeing the clear, clean waters of the multitudes of rivers, cooking out on toasty warm campfires, and cheerfully insulting each other about their lives back in high school. This year in particular promised a huge celebration as Ben and his wife excitedly awaited a new baby, Stewart just got promoted, Robby finally scored season tickets for his basketball team, and Josh recently recovered from a broken leg; sometimes life could almost burst for reasons of celebrating.

Ben and Josh arrived first and began airing out the cabin, unloading supplies and gathering piles of firewood. Usually Robby and Stewart arrived in time to help, but they seemed to be running a bit late that year. The brothers decided to move out to the back deck with a couple of sodas to wait for them. No other cabins existed for miles, so they'd have no trouble hearing the guys pull into the drive.

After a couple of hours had passed with the setting sun lighting the tree's leaves aglow, the brothers became a bit uneasy. Robby and Stewart had never run this late before, and the brothers had begun to worry. But just then, they heard the familiar and ragged muffler of Robby's truck roar around the curve and settle into silence in the drive. The sound of Stewart's voice commenting on the fall colors drifted over on the breeze.

"Hey guys!" Josh hollered. "It's about time. We're out back."

Ben and Josh waited, but then heard nothing. Thinking Stewart and Robby decided to play a prank, the brothers got up to investigate. They rounded the side of the cabin and found the driveway empty.

"I could have sworn I'd heard Stewart's voice," Josh muttered.

"And Robby's truck racket is unmistakable. They were definitely here, so where'd they go?"

Before Josh could reply, his cell phone spouted off its annoying ring tone. He pulled it out of his pocket and answered. "Hello?"

Ben watched in confusion as the color drained from his brother's face. Josh ended the call without saying goodbye, slowly sinking down on the step in shock.

"That was Robby's mom. Robby and Stewart had a car accident two hours ago. They're dead."

ECHOS OF THE ONTONAGON LIGHT

Lighthouses have guided many a sailor along the vast shores of Lake Superior, giving direction, offering hope, providing a secure hand throughout the long, dark nights and the abrasive, wailing storms. And beside every bright, shining lighthouse has stood her keeper, brave and true, dedicated and consistent. Although the job of lighthouse keeper has mostly faded into the past, many of those heroic spirits linger on today, continuing in their unending quest to ensure safety to the shores of Superior.

The Ontonagon Lighthouse is a prime example of such enduring spirits. She has hosted a long line of keepers and their families throughout her century long era of guarding and guiding the Ontonagon harbor. One particular keeper, a Mr. Tom Stripe, had an extra challenge in completing his duties --- Mr. Stripe only had one arm. He lost his left arm in a bar room brawl that resulted in a constant and painful reminder of that day for the rest of his life. But he bravely kept his post at the lighthouse, making adaptations when necessary. For example, keepers often had to carry a large, five-gallon container of lamp oil up the narrow, circular staircase to reach the lamp room. This task proved to be a bit unbalancing for the one-armed Mr. Stripe. He compensated by taking it slow, easy and one step at a time; he would hoist the lamp oil up one step, set it down, then take the step with his feet, then hoist the oil up another step, etc. As this process had to be completed many times throughout the night, it most likely proved tiresome, but Mr. Stripe never complained; he bravely completed his keeper duties every day and every night throughout his entire term. And some say he continues to complete his keeper duties to this day.

One specific witnessing of Mr. Stripe occurred off-hours to one of the Ontonagon County Historical Society members. While the Ontonagon Lighthouse beam hasn't shone for quite awhile, she is open for tours. The Ontonagon County Historical Society is dedicated to restoring and sharing this wonderful piece of history to all who are interested. In the past, before purchasing flood lights, they would decorate the lighthouse with strands of holiday lights. Late one evening, a member of the historical society noticed that a few of the bulbs had blown, so he drove over with some spares to repair it. He entered through the lower hall, and in his haste, tripped over the five-gallon lamp oil container left there for display. A methodical man, he set the container back in place, and then climbed the circular stairway to the lamp room. From there, he stepped out onto the catwalk to reach where the lights hung. The wind moaned and howled that night, as if haunted with the spirits of sailors long dead. The

fellow from the Historical Society pulled his coat closed, clutched tight to the railing and quickly inspected the string of lights. Luckily, he found the blown bulbs within a few minutes and soon reentered the quiet air of the lamp room. He took a moment to catch his breath, but before he could descend the steps, he heard a loud "Thump!"

"Hello? Is anyone there?" Maybe more lights had blown, and another member of the Historical Society had come to tell him. No answer.

"Bruce?" he called. "Is that you? Did I forget something?"

"Thump!"

The man tried to think; did he lock the door behind him when he entered? Yes, he's positive he locked the door; he always locked the door. Then who could be making that noise? The man's heart pounded faster, and despite the chilly air, sweat dripped from his brow. He cleared his throat.

"Um, hello? Who's there?"

"Thump!"

He took a deep breath, steadied his shoulders, and descended down the steps. After all, what danger could there be in an empty lighthouse? That's what he tried to tell himself anyway. Down the spiral staircase he slowly went, one hand on the rail for balance, the other clutching the spare flashlight he always carried just in case. Then he caught sight of something that stopped him cold, sending chills down his spine. Sitting on the second floor landing was the five-gallon lamp oil container, the same one he'd tripped over in the first floor hallway! It

seems the one-armed keeper Mr. Stripe was still working hard, thumping his way up the stairs carrying the lamp oil container to feed the light.

* * *

Another heroic keeper by the name of Mr. James Corgan actually saved the Ontonagon Lighthouse from being consumed in a horrendous fire. In August of 1896, small wildfires blazed up in the bogs surrounding the village of Ontonagon. The village didn't concern herself too much by these fires as they seemed to be keeping their distance. But on the fateful day of Tuesday, August 25, the winds shifted direction and forced the fire right into Ontonagon. Constructed mostly of wood-framed buildings, the

village never stood a chance. Even more fuel for the fire sat in the lumberyard of the Diamond Match Company. The wildfire fed well that day, and hungry for more, she stormed straight for the lighthouse!

Mr. Corgan, ever vigilant on his post, had been watching the fire progress. Time had come to act, to save the lighthouse! Armed with only buckets and their courage, Mr. Corgan, his wife, a daughter and the kitchen maid scurried down to the water's edge. Bucket by bucket, they hauled the life-saving water up the spiral staircase to soak the roof. Blisters formed and burst on their hands; bare feet scorched and burned on the hot sand; lungs gasped for oxygen in the smoky air, yet the brave Corgans never gave up and never left their post. Even with the wildfire toasting their toes and licking at the foundation, they continued the fight. At about four o'clock in the afternoon, just when the fire prepared to swallow the lighthouse, a blessed change

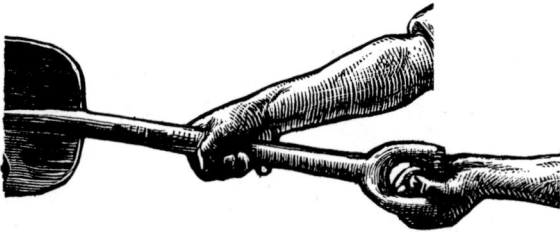

in the wind forced the fire in the other direction. The lighthouse survived!

The dedication and bravery of those four people can still be witnessed, years after their heroic deed. Every seven years, when August 25 falls again on a Tuesday, a person can climb up to the tower at about four o'clock in the afternoon, and witness an echo of their heroic actions replayed --- in the shadows splayed in the yard! No one stands on the roof, yet clearly one can see the shadows continue on in the valiant battle to save the lighthouse from the flames!

DREAMS DESTROYED

April 27, 1857 started out like most every other day for John Floyd. He woke to the cheerful chatter of the goldfinches and chickadees at his home in Rockland, Michigan. The young immigrant prepared for work and then set out, whistling an old tune from his homeland. John worked as a miner in the Minesota Copper Mine, and that's Minesota spelled with only one 'n'. John enjoyed his job well enough, despite it being dirty and dangerous, yet the true highlight of his day came after work when John walked the four miles down the road to a neighboring mine's boarding house in order to visit

his sweetheart. They planned to get married just as soon as they had saved up a bit of money.

But no matter how much he enjoyed thinking about their wonderful life together, John knew that when he reached the mine, he couldn't let his mind wander with daydreams about their happy future together. For John knew he had to concentrate totally and completely on the task at hand. His life and the lives of his co-workers depended on it.

John Floyd and his partner John Nicholas made up part of the blasting team for the Minesota Mine. The dangerous process began with the miners making their way into the dark, dismal depths of the hillside. The partners proceeded to drill three holes into the rock, and then add blasting powder and fuses. The fuses would be lit and the miners quickly evacuated. The impending

explosion blasts into the solid wall, crumbling the rock and copper into pieces. After the dust settles, the miners return to pick through the rubble for the valuable copper chunks. But before further holes

44

can be drilled, the men must first search for any dud fuses that didn't burn. No man wanted to miss leftover powder, for if the next holes drilled produced a spark, it could blow up in his face and he could say goodbye to this world (nor worry about having put on clean under britches that morning).

As John and his partner made their way in the dusty mine for the second time that day, John accidentally forgot the rule of always staying focused. He chatted excitedly about some new plans he and his sweetheart had made; if they could save up enough money they hoped to be able to travel back to his homeland and introduce his new bride to his family. In his distracted chatter, the men overlooked an unlit fuse.

The explosion shook the mine and pandemonium let lose. Rescuers rushed in to pull both Johns from the rubble. The partners had survived the blast, but only just barely. John Nicholas died a few hours later at the hospital. John Floyd only lived twenty minutes after being carried to the surface. The blast had taken off half of his face.

When John's sweetheart heard the news that her fiancé had died, she refused to believe it. For years she kept a lighted lantern glowing in her window, waiting for him to show. And it seems John himself refused to believe his death as well. He continues to spend his evenings walking the route to his beloved. Witnesses see a man dressed in miner's garb wandering down Highway 45 near Rockland. When the witnesses pull up along side of him, he never speaks, but will slowly turn and look at them --- a man with only half a face!

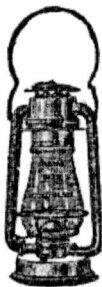

HAUNTED HOTEL

The Landmark Inn opened her doors in 1930 under the original name of The Hotel Northland. Located at 230 North Front Street in Marquette, Michigan, The Landmark Inn has hosted quite a few celebrates in her classically beautiful rooms, including Amelia Earhart, Abbot and Costello, Louis Armstrong and the singing trio Peter, Paul and Mary. She has also hosted a few guests who have decided to stay for all eternity.

Miss Katie lived by herself, but she was rarely alone. As Marquette's librarian, Miss Katie spent her days reading stories to eager children, helping students research presidents and pine squirrels, filling in

blanks on family trees for budding ancestral hunters, and in general passing on her love of books to anyone she met. But despite the constant crowd of visitors to the library, Miss Katie felt a bit lonely. She'd never met that special someone with whom to marry and share her otherwise contented life. After years of waiting and watching for her soul mate, Miss Katie finally gave up hope, totally involving herself with the library's renovation projects.

One Saturday afternoon just about closing time, Miss Katie noticed a loose shelf in the nonfiction department. As she bent to examine it, the entire shelf gave away and Miss Katie scrambled to grab a hold before it tumbled to the floor. She succeeded in preventing a major disruption, but now she was stuck squatting in the nonfiction section supporting an unruly shelf with no means of escape.

"Um, hello," she called out softly, for who knows better than a librarian the importance of silence. But she didn't hold much hope for rescue as the library appeared deserted this late in the afternoon. Was she destined to hold the weight of the shelf until opening hours the next day?

Then a figure appeared around the aisle, the setting sun pouring in through the window setting a highlighting glow about him. "You appear as if you could use some assistance."

"Oh, yes, please!" And together they emptied the shelf of nonfiction books and gently set down the misbehaving shelf.

"You know," he said, studying the situation, "I believe a few well-placed screws would fix that shelf." He slipped next door to the hardware store and quickly returned with a handful of screws and a screwdriver. Soon, the shelf stood sturdy once again, and Miss Katie had developed an endearing crush on the stranger.

In no time, the couple became happily engaged, though they did have one small obstacle to overcome. Miss Katie's fiancé lived in Wisconsin. He had wandered into the library while in town on business with his iron ore company. But they soon decided he would go back home, pack his belongings and quickly return to begin their lives together in Marquette, starting with a wedding and a honeymoon in the lovely Landmark Inn. Miss Katie bid farewell to her fiancé, and then checked into the Landmark Inn in room 604, better known as the lilac room, to await his return.

Every day Miss Katie would call down to the front desk for news of her fiancés return, and every day the patient receptionist would reply with no news. Until one day news finally did await her --- her fiancé's ship had sunk in the turbulent waters of Lake Superior with no survivors.

Miss Katie never did leave room 604, and not long after receiving the horrific news, poor Miss Katie died of a lonely, broken heart. And to this day, she awaits in the Lilac Room for her fiancé's return.

When the Landmark Inn recently reopened after being closed for renovations, a gentleman staying in room 604 found a handful of screws in the bed. He reported his findings and then went downstairs for dinner. Housekeeping held the recent renovations responsible for the overlooked screws, and quickly remade his bed with fresh sheets. Upon returning for the night, the gentleman guest found another handful of screws in his bed.

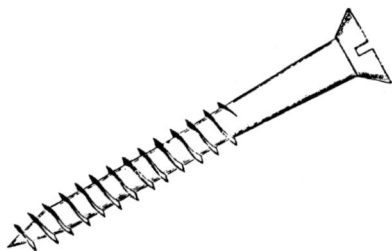

And the phone calls originating from the Lilac room still ring in regularly at the front desk, even when room 604 is empty.

AND THE CHILDREN CRY

The Keweenaw Peninsula juts proudly out into Lake
Superior about halfway across the northern shore of the U.P. This
part of the Upper Peninsula is
even more wild and isolated,
topping the records with 390
inches of snow in 1978-79!
That's 32.5 *feet*! So getting
out and about during the
winter months proved
challenging to say the least.
It took an exciting event, say
a Christmas musical program, to entice the town folk of Calumet
out in the frigid cold and deep snows. The entire town eagerly
gathered at the Italian Hall on Christmas Eve in 1913, to enjoy an

evening of entertainment, unknowing that the festivities would end in a tragic disaster.

The musical program began at seven sharp. The sun had set hours before, yet sparkling stars and a bright sliver of a moon lit the villagers' way through the bitter cold streets. And by half past, the darkened theater literally hummed from beautiful holiday music and a warm, happy audience.

But then, a clumsy baritone tripped on his stage entrance, knocking over an eight-tear candle stand. The bright flames grabbed greedily at the edge of the velvet curtains, igniting the edge of the stage! The clumsy baritone acted quickly, stomping on the flames with his size 14 dance shoes, halting the fire's insatiable feast. But the damage had ignited.

"Fire!"

Women screamed, men cursed and children cried as the panicked crowd raced for the exit. The slow moving, cane-wielding Grandfather Soady tripped in the confusion, knocking little Sara over on

his way down. Nobody saw them fall in the dimmed theater; no one knew to help them back on their feet. Pandemonium ruptured as the audience crowded at the exit doors --- doors that opened inward. They flooded the closed exits like a river against a dam, unable to escape. In the mass darkness, confusion and panic, 73 men, women and children died that night from suffocation and trampling.

The Italian Hall has since been torn down, but a memorial stands so that no one will ever forget. And to this day, on the anniversary of their deaths, children's voices can be heard near the memorial, voices crying out for help, crying out to be remembered.

SCHOOL SPIRIT

Jeffers High boasts lots of school spirit, and not just for their sports teams! Located in Painesdale off of Highway M-26, Jeffers High opened in the late 1800's and is named after the superintendent Mr. Fred Jeffers who carefully monitored the halls for over fifty years. Many, including a few eye witnesses, claim he continues to roam the halls today!

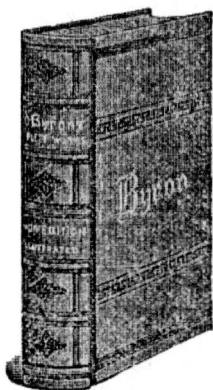

During a recent, routine inspection, the town's fire chief insisted that the upper floor be cleared of possible fire hazards. The attic had long served as storage for outdated textbooks, old student files, faded school board meeting minutes and records. But it all had to go in order to comply with the fire codes. So the very next day, the head janitor climbed the stairs, unlocked the attic door and started in on the mess. Load after load he hauled down to his pickup truck, until all that remained were the boxes piled in front of the window. The janitor, Mr. Weaser, hesitated to just toss out such seemingly historical documents. After all, Mr. Jeffers' signature and

handwriting peppered many of the pages. But the janitor had his instructions. He carried those boxes down to his truck as well, and then drove to the landfill. He dumped the entire load and then returned to the school. Deed done.

A few days later, the principal called the head janitor into his office.

"Mr. Weaser, I wondered when you meant to finish clearing out the attic. We need to have it finished before the fire chief returns."

"Oh, I finished that up days ago," Mr. Weaser assured the principal.

"Well, I'm afraid we have a disagreement on the word 'finished'," objected the principal, "because I climbed the steps to the attic just this morning, and boxes still line the wall."

"But, I swear, I cleared the room days ago…"

The janitor and principal together went to inspect the attic. They unlocked the door and swung it open. There sitting in a dusty sunbeam shining through the window sat the very boxes Mr. Weaser had removed!

The only explanation they could come up with pointed blame to a mischievous student playing a prank. Though neither could explain how the student got past the locked door.

Shaking his head, the principal assisted the janitor in hauling the boxes down to his truck. Mr. Weaser drove back to the landfill, but this time dumped the boxes into the hopper and watched the flames consume them down to ash. Deed done, again. Yet a few days later, when the janitor and principal escorted the fire chief back to inspect the attic, the boxes had mysteriously returned, stacked back beneath the window! The principal and head janitor tried to explain the unexplainable situation to the fire chief. The slightly superstitious fire chief decided that since the remaining boxes didn't clutter up the attic too much, they could stay; he signed the inspection report. The boxes still sit stacked beneath the window today.

* * *

Another janitor had a rather spine-tingling encounter in the darkened, pre-dawn hours of Jeffers High School. Mr. Fayette had just finished checking the boiler, part of his morning routine, and made his way back to the offices by way of cutting through the gymnasium. He'd walked this path hundreds of time, and didn't bother flipping the switch to light his way. The gym always sat empty at that time of the morning.

But then, off to his left, he heard the dribbling of a basketball echoing into the empty caverns of the gym. At first, the unexpected sound startled the janitor, but then he realized that a student must have snuck in early to shoot some hoops.

"Hey there," Mr. Fayette called out. "You know you're not supposed to be in here before hours."

No response, just the methodical bouncing of the basketball.

A bit disgruntled, Mr. Fayette marched over to the bank of lights and flooded the gym.

No one was there, just a lone basketball lying motionless against the wall.

Great, he thought, *now I'll have to comb the hallways looking for the kid.* Irritated, he flipped the lights off and started back across the gym.

BOING...BOING...BOING. Someone began bouncing the ball again.

"Okay," he muttered, "I've about had enough—" He stormed back over to the wall and jerked the light switch.

The room remained eerily empty --- except now the basketball lay motionless in the middle of the floor!

Mr. Fayette had about enough foolishness. He turned the lights off again, but this time he stood next to the switch. Sure enough, the basketball dribbling started. The bouncing drew near to where he stood by the wall, closer and closer. Mr. Fayette waited, poised to catch the prankster in the act. He held his breath, paused for just the right moment and...

"Gotcha!"

Chills ran down Mr. Fayette's spine. The room stood completely empty except for a motionless basketball laying not five inches from his feet!

Mr. Fayette hurried from the gym, with the lights left burning.

* * *

Mrs. Nelson also worked at Jeffers High School. As the head cook in the cafeteria, she often came in early to get a head start. The talented Mrs. Nelson reached way beyond the minimum

job specifications of providing lunch; she pleased students and faculty alike with her mouth-watering desserts, crusty breads and fruit-filled pastries.

So one morning, just like every other morning, Mrs. Nelson stumbled into the cloakroom, brushing off the freshly fallen snow clinging to her tightly permed curls and kicking her boots free of the collected ice and mud. As she turned to hang up her coat, movement caught her eye through the wavy-glassed door that led to the kitchen.

Strange, she thought, *no one else usually comes in this early.*

But when she opened the door, the shadowed kitchen appeared normal, devoid of human activities so early in the A.M.

Wondering what had snatched her attention, Mrs. Nelson closed the door again and glanced through the wavy glass.

Yes, there! Standing by the stoves stood a large man who appeared to be inspecting the equipment.

"Excuse me," Mrs. Nelson called out as she pulled open the door. "May I help y—"

She stopped mid-sentence, as her voice echoed off into the empty kitchen. "Strange," she murmured as the hairs prickled at the base of her neck. She closed the door but didn't latch it, keeping her hand on the knob. She glanced through the glass

again, this time a bit more cautious. At first she didn't see anything.

"Hmm, maybe it's time to visit the eye doctor," she mumbled as she leaned in close and peered through the wavy glass. "It has been over two years—"

A shadowed face pressed up against the glass, glaring back at her!

Mrs. Nelson screamed and turned to run, accidentally yanking the door open in her hast. In a panic, she looked over her shoulder for the intruder, expecting to see him on her heels, but the kitchen was empty!

Mrs. Nelson never again entered Jeffers High School alone.

A VISIT FROM AN ANGEL

A young woman by the name of Jenny had just received devastating news --- she had been diagnosed with a brain tumor. The doctors predicted a twenty percent survival rate with surgery, and a zero percent chance without. But even with the surgery, she could end up blind or deaf. The situation didn't look good, and Jenny had to make some very tough decisions. As the mother of two young boys, she worried about their future. If she died, and the odds didn't look very promising, who would care for her children? She turned to her parents,

the boys' grandparents, and did one of the hardest things she's ever had to do, handed over custody to them. That way, if she died, the boys would be well cared for. With her worst fears covered, she turned to start the biggest fight on her life --- her very survival.

Chemotherapy hadn't been going well; Jenny felt drained and excruciatingly sick, and it didn't even appear to be affecting the tumor. So the doctors planned surgery for the following Monday morning. On Sunday afternoon, Jenny entered Saint Francis Hospital in Escanaba, Michigan. By nine P.M., she lay alone in the room, her thoughts on the next day's surgery.

Then near the end of her bed, a figure in white appeared. The figure radiated a feeling of peace, almost a physical glow emanating around her body. Jenny stared in wonder.

"You will be healed," the figure spoke in a soft, soothing voice. Then she disappeared.

Almost immediately, Jenny felt free from pain.

The next morning, the doctors arrived to perform a spinal tap in order to relieve the extra pressure in her brain. The pressure had to be as low as possible to perform the surgery. But as they examined the charts and monitors, the doctors started murmuring to each other excitedly.

"This is strange," one commented.

"Almost unheard of," another exclaimed.

The pressure in Jenny's brain had dropped back to normal, and they cancelled the surgery. The doctors had no medical reasons to explain why the danger had disappeared. Jenny knew why --- the visit from the angel had saved her life.

UNINVITED VISITORS

Linda is a snowbird, meaning she spends her summers in Eagle River, Michigan, enjoying the peaceful forests, the shy and secretive wildlife, and the miles of pristine shoreline along the beautiful Lake Superior, and then in the winter, she lives someplace else, enjoying temperatures that don't dwell below zero and landscapes that aren't blanketed by three feet of snow. Her house in the U.P. is over 140 years old, but sturdily built with lots of life left in it, and in more ways than one.

In the fall, as the temperatures begin to drop, as the frost clings to the morning air, as the geese fly south and the all-over-greens begin shifting to reds, golds and browns, Linda closes up her house for the winter months. She drains the water pipes, unplugs the appliances, bolts the windows and secures the doors. Every year she asks the sheriff to do an occasional drive by, just to check on the house to make sure everything is okay. And almost every year the sheriff is forced to call Linda. He has to inform her that even though she and he have the only sets of keys, her previously locked house is ajar, that every door and every window gapes wide open! It's almost as if someone doesn't wish to be locked up and forgotten during the dark and cold months.

And was it that same spirit who decided he didn't like the prepped fireplace? Linda had recently remodeled the sitting room with a brick facelift and new glass doors for the huge fireplace. She finished it off by laying a picturesque fire, complete with peeling birch logs, pine cones and red-berried twigs, all but the actual flames. Linda purposely left the tight

fitting glass doors open to show off her handiwork. Then she went upstairs to check on her sleeping grandson. When she returned, the sight of the sitting room stunned her into silence. The fireplace lay empty, not a twig or curl of birch bark remained, and the doors stood firmly closed. The birch logs now lay neatly stacked beneath the window and the decorative pine cones and twigs lay in tidy piles on the table!

Linda's mysterious house guest also moves picture frames and knick knacks around from room to room. He doesn't seem to have any ill wish for Linda and her family; he just seems to have his own style of decorating.

GHOST DRIVER

Harold found himself caught unexpectedly in a frigid, autumn downpour, putting a damper on his evening walk to the bar just inside of Kenton, Michigan. The cold rain puddled on the warm ground creating wisps of ghost-like fog rising and waltzing into the night air. Harold quickened his pace, but with the cold and damp, his arthritis flared in protest making movement more difficult. So when he spotted a pair of headlights glowing around the curve behind him, he stuck out his thumb to flag it down for a ride.

The old, rusty car rolled to a stop, and Harold gratefully climbed inside. He slammed the door closed, and then turned to thank the driver --- but there was no one there!

"*That's strange*," Harold thought, peering through the rain-spattered windows for the driver. *Where'd he go?*

But before he could investigate further, the car began to move, and with no one in the driver's seat!

The car crept down the deserted road, the headlights barely piercing the black, foggy night. Startled at the now runaway car, Harold latched a death grip onto the dashboard and frantically searched the murky darkness for the missing driver. But then a glimpse of an upcoming curve shook Harold from his stupor. The car would surely run off the road and plummet down into the gully to burst into a flaming fireball! He had to escape and fast!

He reached for the door handle, but a movement caught his eye, freezing his entire body in fear. A ghostly hand appeared out of nowhere, a

hand with no body! The grizzled hand, bent and wrinkled and coated with black slime, reached into the car and clamped onto the steering wheel. The car maneuvered the curve safely and continued on its path. Shocked into near panic, Harold froze in his seat, unable to move except for the erratic pounding of his heart. He sat like a stone statue, trapped in the car with a ghost!

Together, the silent disembodied ghost and the terrified old man traveled down the gravel road. Once or twice, Harold tried to communicate with the ghost, asking him or her to just pull over so that he could get out. But the ghost either could not, or chose not to answer. Just as Harold had decided to leap from the moving car,

the ghost pulled over to the side of the road. Harold wasted no time, wrenching open the door and stumbling to safety! He ran as fast as his trembling, arthritic knees could carry him, not stopping until he collapsed on a bar stool surrounded by his friends.

As he related the terrifying experience, his friends had a hard time believing the incredible tale, yet none could dispel the cold sweat on Harold's brow or the look of fear glinting in his eye.

A few minutes later, the front door swung open, and two men in black oilskin coats stepped inside, bringing with them a gust of frozen, foggy air and leaving puddles on the floor.

"Hey look, Charlie," one of the strangers pointed at Harold. "It's that crazy old man who climbed in our stalled car as we were pushing it down the road!"

WAR WOUNDS

Jesse and Jasper have always done everything together, from milking cows on the farm, taking the first bone-chilling dip of every year in Lake Superior, to stealing the ripe, ruby red apples from grumpy old man Peter's orchard. They even shared a womb together. They looked exactly alike, and everyone in the village of Escanaba confused the identical twins. Once Jasper's girl, Ellen, even snuck behind the one-roomed school house to surprise him with a kiss, and accidentally surprised the wrong brother; not that Jesse minded overly much.

The twins' mother always bragged that God had made such a perfect human being that He just had to make two of them. Practically the entire village agreed with her; everybody adored the twins (except for old man Peters). Which made it all the harder when Jesse and Jasper signed up with the Union's 27th infantry of Michigan volunteers to fight in the Civil War.

A year later, both of the twins had promoted to corporal, with quite a bit of experience in the battlefield. Like most everyone else, the twins longed for home, but the war was far from finished. Jasper had just been handed a secret assignment that would take him into the mountains of Virginia. The night before Jasper left, Jesse reluctantly bid him farewell; Jesse had a bad feeling about the excursion, but didn't confide his forebodings with his brother. Jasper had enough on his mind with just completing the mission and staying alive. He didn't need a worrisome brother distracting him with cold feet.

The first few days passed uneventfully for Jesse. He kept busy running drills with the other soldiers in their temporary camp at the edge of the Tennessee/Virginia border. But on day four, Jesse woke in the pre-dawn hours with an excruciating pain shooting up his right arm, almost as if an explosion erupted beneath his skin. He stumbled out of his tent, clutching his arm in agony, and fell to the ground breathlessly. Gradually, the pain did begin to lesson, until it suddenly disappeared altogether leaving his right arm completely numb. When Jesse's mind cleared, he knew without a doubt that Jasper needed help. He couldn't explain how he knew or what kind of trouble Jasper had fallen into, he only understood that he had to find him.

Without telling his tent neighbors or even his captain, Jesse stole out of camp on one of the cavalry's bay geldings. Galloping through the shadowy, early mourning hours, Jesse clung to the sweating horse, his right arm still unexplainably numb. He had no idea where

Jasper had gone, but his gut instinct led him into the Tennessee mountains, right on Jasper's trail.

Some time later, with his sturdy steed nearing exhaustion, Jesse dismounted at a sparkling creek running through a quiet meadow. Leaving the horse to rest, Jesse continued on foot. Feeling his brother's presence, Jesse crept stealthily though the forested grove, smelling the thick woody scent of smoke and feeling the icy clutch of death in the air. A clearing opened up revealing a homestead in the smoky mists of burning to the ground. Two bodies lay dead in the yard, musket wounds to the head and chest. Jesse barely glanced at them; somehow he knew his brother lay in the farthest barn, the one still standing, the one with flames licking at the door.

Jessie ran to the burning building and bravely reached for the doors. But no amount of bravery could overcome the red hot flames and scorching heat that engulfed the barn entrance. Helplessly, Jesse paced back and forth, unwilling to let his brother die, yet unable to get inside. In utter frustration, he

punched the solid barn wall, being suddenly reminded of his numbed right hand. A numbed hand wouldn't felt the pain of fire, the burning and searing of flesh! Jesse tried again, this time using his numbed hand to pry open the burning doors. Through the thick black smoke, he could see a pile of fallen timbers in the corner. The hungry fire jumped onto that feast of wood just as Jesse caught sight of his brother's leg sticking out from beneath it. He dove in like a crazed man, pulling off the burning, red hot timbers with his numbed hand, not stopping to think of the appalling damage he caused to himself. With just seconds to spare, Jesse unburied his twin and hauled Jasper to safety as the burning barn collapsed into a pile of flaming ruins.

Within a few hours, both brothers lay in hospital beds, suffering extensive injuries and badly burned, but alive. It turns out that Jasper had stumbled into a trap during his secret mission. A carefully planned explosion narrowly missed taking his life, but definitely managed to take off his arm at the elbow, his right arm---

the same arm and at the same time that Jesse had felt that intense pain back at the camp. How had Jesse felt his twin's pain from miles away? How had he known how to find Jasper? The bond between identical twins is a mystery. And even after Jasper lost his right arm in the explosion, identical twins they continued to be. Jesse's own right arm had to be amputated at the elbow from the extensive damage suffered in the daring rescue of his brother.

MANSFIELD MINE DISASTER

The Mansfield Mine bustled with iron ore extraction during the 1890's. The entrance sat along the west bank of the Michigamme River in Iron County, with her six levels of shafts reaching 428 feet down into the earth beneath the river. The miners, mostly immigrants, toiled through the dangerous tasks of harvesting the mine for only about $1.50 per day. By 1893, the hard working miners had just about cleared shafts one through five of the valuable ore, leaving behind only the support system of columns and timbers to brace the weight of the overhanging rock.

On the evening of September 27, 1893, crew supervisor Frank Rocko arrived at the Mansfield Mine for his late shift. He

and his crew climbed down to the fourth shaft to finish clearing out the ore remains, while another crew continued down to begin work on the sixth shaft. A total of forty-eight men had descended the mine that night, when the disastrous collapse occurred. Level five's supports cracked and splintered under the weight of the upper levels, caving in onto itself. Realizing what happened, miners in shaft six immediately started for the surface. By the time they reached shaft four, water from the Michigamme River had started pouring into the mine. The miners continued up the ladders, battling

against the incoming rush of water, but Frank Rocko refused to go with them. He bravely ran off into the dark, disintegrating shaft to warn his crew. Sadly, Frank and his miners never made it to the surface. In fact, of the forty-eight men in the mine that night, only twenty made it out alive.

Frank Rocko is a hero, sacrificing his own life in trying to save the lives of his crew. Some say Frank's spirit continues on in his quest to warn the miners of shaft four. Witnesses have reported seeing him wandering the west bank of the Michigamme River, lantern held high, voice wailing out in warning, only to disappear into the misty fog rising from the waters.

.

MOTHER OF THE LIGHT

Anastasia Eliza Truckey dropped down on a log to remove her shoes. Freeing her toes to the early morning breeze felt like Heaven, and she tilted back her head to catch the sun's warm touch on her face. Lake Superior lay calm and sleepy after last night's torrential storm of howling winds, thundering waves and drenching rain. Anastasia had stood vigil though the long hours making sure the lighthouse had burned bright and steady, never once going out. Keeping the Marquette Lighthouse operating was Anastasia's job, and she took it very seriously. Even more so since her husband, Nelson Truckey, had left to fight for the Union in the

war, leaving the once shared responsibilities entirely to her. Though she missed him dreadfully and worried about him constantly, she did love her work and took tremendous pride in being one of the first woman lighthouse keepers on The Great Lakes.

Anastasia wiggled her toes down into the sun-warmed sands, enjoying her few moments of peace before returning to the lighthouse. Soon her children would awaken and be clamoring for breakfast. And then she needed to start on the baking, and the laundry pile hadn't shrunk on its own like she'd hoped when wishing on that shooting star last week.

She stood and stretched, groaning as her back cracked in relief. The chores would get done eventually, and then there'd be plenty more to take their place. Once the children finished their studies, they'd help out, bringing their songs and smiles and stories along with their helping hands, making the time pass with pleasure. She turned to walk back to the lighthouse, but then stumbled back, shaken at the presence of a stranger.

"Oh," she gasped, "you startled me!"

"Forgive me, Mother of the Light."

"That's quite all right; I was floating off in my own little world." She studied the Indian curiously. He stood maybe five foot six, but not for a moment did Anastasia question his authority. Proud and confident with buckskin breeches, bald eagle feathers in his long, mostly white hair, and a bear claw necklace around his sun-weathered neck. A nasty red scar crossed his face from chin to brow, crossing over his left eye leaving it milky-white and sightless. And he'd called her Mother of the Light.

She smiled in warm welcome. "Only one group of people calls me that. You must be part of the Ojibwa Indian tribe on the other side of the Marquette Village."

The man nodded, returning her smile. "They are my family. And it is because of them that I've come today. I have need to ask a favor of you."

Surprised, but also curious, Anastasia replied, "If I am able, I would be honored."

He dipped his head in thanks, and then removed the necklace, the twenty dangerous-looking bear claws

strung on a piece of leather. "Please take this to my people. It must rest in their hands before the next full moon."

Anastasia took the necklace, feeling a shocking zap as her fingers brushed his. "I will go this afternoon."

"Mother of the Light, I thank you." He turned and walked into the forest, disappearing from sight.

The afternoon had clouded over, threatening another storm, but Anastasia didn't put off her assigned task. Something in the Indian's voice had professed urgency, even though everything else about him indicated a deep calm. She urged her horse into a soft cantor, checking her pocket yet again for the bear claw necklace.

She'd visited the Ojibwa Indian tribe once before, when her visiting, out-of-town cousin had gotten himself in a bit of trouble with the Ojibwa's, and had almost lost his life. Still, it took a bit of searching to find the correct path again. She soon stood at the edge of the village, face to face with the Ojibwa tribe. They welcomed her to their home.

As soon as the greetings concluded, Anastasia got right to the point of her visit. "One of your people asked me to bring you this." She held out the beautiful necklace.

A collective gasp rounded the group at the sight of the necklace, followed by fast, excited talking. One fellow reached out, hesitated, and then carefully took the necklace into his hands.

"Where did you get this, Mother of the Light?"

Anastasia told them about the Indian she'd met on the beach, what he'd said, describing him from snowy-white head to moccasin-clad toe. When she reached the part about the horrible scar and useless eye, the crowd grew deathly quiet.

"What's wrong?" she asked nervously, a foreboding feeling taking root in her stomach.

The fellow held out the necklace for all to see. "This necklace has been passed down from leader to leader as far back as our stories go. It is very important to the history of our people. We believed it to be lost forever when four years ago it burned

down to ash in a horrendous fire, along with our beloved leader ---
the very man you just described."

LONG-TERM GUESTS

A lovely bed and breakfast in Calumet, Michigan often welcomes a certain guest who does not require a reservation. The owners make an exception for this fellow, as he was the original guest of the house --- back in 1873!

Pat, the owner, first encountered the guest in the living room. Silhouetted against the enticing flames, a gentleman in 19th century attire leaned against the fireplace mantle. He didn't say anything; he just stood gazing into the fire while chewing on the end of his unlit pipe.

Pat blinked to clear her vision, and the ghost disappeared.

Determined to discover the truth of her mysterious guest, Pat visited the library to conduct a little research. Buried in the musty log books of the village's past, Pat found a photograph of a Mr. Henry Brett. Mr. Brett had been the first person to live in her bed and breakfast, originally built in 1873 by a mining company to house employees. The image of Mr. Brett matched exactly to the mysterious visitor who had stood in her living room just a day earlier!

On another afternoon, Pat went upstairs to check on her granddaughter. The two-year-old stood at the crib's edge with an outstretched hand calling 'Kitty, kitty, kitty!' Pat followed the child's gaze to the corner, but there was nothing there, at least as far as she could see anyway.

This bed and breakfast's unusual guests never seem to mean any mischief or harm, so they are always welcome. After all, it is their home, too.

INCESSANT DEDICATION

Old Victoria Falls in Rockland, Michigan exists as a living museum to showcase the lives of miners during the massive iron ore and copper mining operations in the U.P. during the 1800 and 1900's. Included in the compound is the Arvola House, home of the dedicated Madam Victoria. The wife of a miner, Madam Victoria, as she became known, kept busy running a boarding house for the mining company, cleaning and preparing food for the mine workers. She met an unfortunate end in 1904, bleeding to death from an injury, leaving behind four young children. But nothing, not even death has kept her from completing her tasks at the boarding house.

Several eyewitnesses of Madam Victoria's continued presence occurred when a local seventh grade class embarked on a three day field trip to the Old Victoria Falls museum to experience life in the late 1800's-early 1900's. The kids dressed the part, cooked the part, slept the part and even used the time period's outhouse. As the class was sitting down to the evening meal, one teacher filled his plate and joined them at the benched table. Everyone shoveled in the food, barely taking the time to chew in between bursts of laughter and the constant streams of chatter. Then the teacher looked up and watched with curiosity as the five kids directly across from him paused, utensils frozen in midair halfway to their gaping mouths, their wide eyes slowly following something moving across the room behind him. The teacher turned to see what had caught his student's attentions in time to see the bedroom door closing shut. Had a breeze blown the door? But surely just a wind wouldn't have caused such a strange reaction from the students. When the startled students could finally speak, they relayed in detail how the front door knob had slowly turned, and

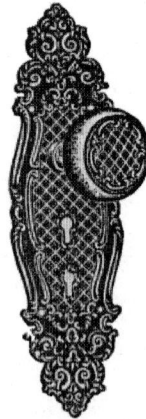

the door had eased opened. Then a ghostly figure draped in a long white dress and gingham apron swept across the room. Then the bedroom door knob had turned and the spirit moved though, closing the door behind her!

Visitors and caretakers alike have witnessed Madame Victoria's presence in various ways, including smelling the wafting scents of cooking food, yet the stove is always cold to the touch, and finding tiny new potatoes in her cabin even in the middle of winter. Others have felt her presence in the rocking chair where she so often sat to stitch up clothes and darn socks. People have seen the seemingly empty chair rock on its own, though no hand nudges it and no breeze blows the air. One visitor has even captured on film the actual levitation of the rocking chair, and that photo is on display at the museum. It seems this dedicated woman will forever continue on in her interrupted life.

THE LONG WALK HOME

The Ontonagon high school football coach peered blindly thought the windshield into the pounding rain. Wipers beat breathlessly against the torrent, but could barely keep up with the storm. The coach slowed the car to a crawl as the fog rolled in, decreasing visibility even more. Sighing in frustration, he reached forward to wipe away the condensation forming on the glass,

when out of the darkness appeared a lone figure walking on the side of the road.

The coach stomped on the brakes and swerved to the left, almost spinning out of control. When the car finally shuddered to a halt, the coach had to close his eyes and gulp a few breaths of air before looking to check on the pedestrian. A young lady appeared at the side window, and the coach leaned over to open the passenger door.

"Are you—" his voice wobbled just a bit, so he cleared his throat. "Are you okay?"

She nodded, cold rain dripping from her hair and into her eyes.

The coach hesitated, and then motioned for her to get in the car. "Let me drive you home. It's the least I can do for almost running you off the road."

"I'd really appreciate it," she murmured with lips blue from the cold. Goose bumps rose all up her bare arms and she shivered uncontrollably in her soaked formal gown.

The coach cranked up the heat sending out blasts of warm air, and then reached into the backseat to grab his team jacket. He handed it to her. "Here, put this on. So, where do you live?"

She motioned down the road while her fingers, clumsy with cold, struggled to pull on the jacket. "Keep going north on 45 past Bruce Crossing, then turn on Two Mile Road."

The coach pulled back onto the wet road and continued driving. After a few moments of silence, he asked "So, what are you doing out here on a night like this?"

At first she just shrugged, staring out into the darkness. When she finally turned back to him, tears mixed with the raindrops streaming down her cheeks. "I had a terrible fight with my boyfriend. We had just left the Ewen-Trout Creek Senior

prom. I had promised my mom I'd come straight home, but Michael wanted to go to a friend's house for a party. It was kinda stupid and all, but the whole thing just got thrown out of whack. Michael ended up kicking me out of the car and then he just drove off without me." She shrugged as she took the offered napkin the coach handed her and dabbed at her smeared eyes. "It was supposed to be the most amazing night of my life, so far anyway. Then I end up having to walk home in the rain, and now I'll probably catch pneumonia and die! And to top it all off, Michael broke up with me!"

The coach allowed her to vent her tears and emotions as he carefully drove her home. He knew teenage girls sometimes tended to over-dramatize, but this girl's evening sounded downright awful. *She's just lucky she didn't get hit on the road*, he thought as he pulled into her driveway.

The young lady thanked him for the ride as she slammed the car door closed. She ran through the rain to the covered front porch where an excited dog welcomed her home. Together they went inside the house.

An hour had passed with the coach pulled into his own driveway before realizing the girl still had his team jacket. Too tired to drive back that night, he decided to stop the next day on his way to the football game.

As it turns out, the coach was running a bit late the next afternoon, and really didn't have the time to spare for reclaiming his jacket, but he couldn't show up at the game without it. So, already impatient and irritated, the coach took the turn back to the girl's house, adding a few extra miles he couldn't afford.

He pulled up into the driveway, noticing how different everything looked rain-washed and sparkling in the bright sunshine. But that sleepy old dog still sat on the porch, climbing stiffly to his feet to

100

greet the coach. He dropped a hand to the hound's head before knocking on the door.

A few seconds passed before the sound of footsteps could be heard. The door opened revealing a woman, worn and tired, yet the coach could see the girl's resemblance in the slightly upturned nose, the angle of her chin and the faded blue eyes; this was definitely the girl's mother.

"Hello! I hate to disturb you, but I need to pick up my jacket."

"Sorry?" The woman stared at him blankly through the screen door.

"Oh, I'm the fellow who gave your daughter a right home last night. Surely she told you about having to walk home in the storm. I stopped and offered her a lift. She was shivering, so I loaned her my jacket, but then she forgot to return it. I need it back."

Tears pooled in the woman's eyes. "I don't think that's funny at all!" She slammed the door.

The coach stood there, his mouth gaping in shock. But anger quickly took over; he didn't have time for other people's lack of communication with their daughters. He pounded on the door.

The door opened immediately. "What do you want?" the woman asked coldly.

"I already told you, I want my jacket back!"

"And I told you that I didn't appreciate your...sense of humor. Go away!

The coach jerked the screen door open. "Listen lady, I don't know what problems you and your daughter have–"

"The problem I have is that my daughter's been dead for twelve years!"

The coach, shocked into silence, stared at the heart-broken woman. When he finally found his voice, he mumbled "Oh, I'm so sorry." His mind raced over the new information. "But then who was the young lady I dropped off last night?"

The woman sighed, opening the door in invitation. "Would you like to come in for a cup of coffee?"

As the coach stepped inside, he noticed a framed photo sitting on a side table. "That's her! That's the girl I dropped off last night!"

The woman choked back a sob, but quickly composed herself. With a handkerchief dabbing her tear-filled eyes, she turned to the coach and studied his confused, yet sincere face. She sighed heavily and then said, "Come with me."

They climbed in his car, and she directed him down some side roads pulling into the Maple Grove Cemetery.

"My daughter's grave," she pointed.

The coach followed her finger and found a lovingly cared for grave site, with neatly trimmed grass and a hanging basket overflowing with colorful flowers. Draped around the granite headstone hung the coach's jacket.

THE FOG AND THE DARKNESS

Late night travelers need always be on wary guard as they drive along the dark and lonely roads in the Upper Peninsula. Beautiful and graceful deer thrive in the U.P.'s habitats, and their populations soar quite high. Each year 10,000 reported deer/car collisions cost millions of dollars in damage, not to mention the priceless casualties of both deer and people. So take caution, drive slowly and keep those eyes open and alert! In addition, drivers on Greenland Road in Ontonagon County need also be on guard

for another creature; some may be lucky enough to catch sight of the ghost jogger!

A few years ago, 22-year-old Jamie set out on his daily run.

Normally he ran his five mile loop in the afternoon while daylight still lit his path. But that particular day had been quite hectic, and Jamie hadn't gotten home until well after dark. Keyed up after a trying day at work, he decided a run would clear his head.

Unfortunately the evening had turned chilly, and a misty fog rose up from the damp pavement. A car barreled around the curve driving way too fast. The driver may have been drunk, or maybe he just didn't see Jamie for the thick fog and star-less night, but the car plowed right over him and didn't even stop. Jamie died almost instantly, alone in the dark.

Sometimes Jamie can be seen, still jogging the Greenland Road. He'll appear in a headlight's beam, usually when a cool mist rises from the darkened

road. And just as it begins to pass, Jamie steps in front of the oncoming car! Terrified drivers feel the sickening thud and slam on the brakes. They leap from the car, their hearts pounding in fear to find…nothing. One or two drivers have even experienced broken headlights or bent grills from their encounters with Jamie. If you find yourself on Greenland Road in Ontonagon County, especially on a cool night with a rising fog, be on the lookout for Jamie and his unending jog into eternity.

SLEEPLESS NIGHTS

Lizzy slammed the door, not caring a whit if she woke up her roommate, Rosa.

"Serves her right," she mumbled as she stormed down the side stairs towards the study cubicles in the lobby. Maybe there she'd be able to get a bit of sleep. Every night since she first arrived in the dormitory at the Northern Michigan University, Lizzy hadn't gotten a decent night's sleep. Why? Because Rosa snored, and not one of those wispy, girlish snores that are kind of cute in babies and dogs, but a deep grumblin' lumberjack gust of a snore that legendarily woke the dead!

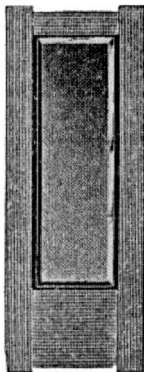

Lizzy found an empty study corner and tried to curl up on one of the ugly-patterned sofas. Of course she'd tried talking to Rosa about the snoring; maybe something could be done to fix the situation. But Rosa swore up and down that she didn't snore, not a whisper. In fact, *she'd* even gotten mad at *Lizzy* for even suggesting such a thing.

As Lizzy slowly calmed down and finally started to drift off to sleep, an idea occurred to her, a way to prove to Rosa that she did indeed snore! Then maybe Rosa would do something about her disruptive problem and Lizzy could finally get some sleep in her own bed.

The next evening when Rosa slipped out to visit the bathroom, Lizzy jumped into action. She pulled out one of those old fashioned tape recorders that she'd borrowed from the Audio/Visual Department, and inserted an old, unused audio tape she'd found at a garage

sale. Slipping the small box-like recorder out of sight beneath Rosa's bed, she pressed down the record button and raced back to her desk just as Rosa returned.

Rosa climbed into bed without a word to Lizzy; she held on to a grudge tighter than a dog to his favorite bone. Lizzy sighed in exasperation, but Rosa would soon be proven wrong --- she did indeed snore, and really, really loudly, too.

Lizzy waited a few moments, feigning her studies, and then quietly excused herself. "I'm going for a soda; want anything?"

Rosa merely rolled over towards the wall, silently shouting rude thoughts.

Lizzy shook her head as she locked the door behind her. Rosa would soon be forced to swallow her rudeness. On her way

back down the hall from the soda machines, she decided to drop in to say hello to the neighbors. She leaned against the door frame while chatting with the two ladies from the south of Georgia, keeping an eye on her own door; she didn't want anyone dropping by to wake Rosa up before she really got into her snoring concerto.

After thirty minutes or so, Lizzy bid the Georgian ladies goodbye and returned to scrutinize the evidence. She carefully and quietly let herself in the room. Sure enough, Rosa snorted and chortled just like usual. Time for Rosa to face the truth! Lizzy slammed the door closed.

"Ha!"

Rosa lurched to the side, falling out of bed. She slowly sat up rubbing her bruised hip. "What the—"

Lizzy strolled over and reached around Rosa to grab the hidden tape recorder. "Now I've got proof that you snore, so much proof that you'll probably be inducted into the snorer's hall of fame!"

"I don't believe you," Rosa grumbled, climbing to her feet. "What are you going to stoop to next? This is an invasion of privacy!"

"Yeah, and you're an invasion of a much needed night's sleep! If I can't get some rest soon, I'll flunk all of my classes! Now you're gonna sit there, listen to the evidence and then admit you snore! And then you're gonna do something about it!"

Lizzy sat at her desk, rewound the tape and then hit play, sending a superior smile over at Rosa.

From the tiny speaker came the static-y noises of rustled movement, a door opening, closing, and then a voice 'I'm going for a soda; want anything?'

Rosa glared, unblinking at Lizzy while the tape rolled forward. Except for some rustlings and mumbled mutterings all seemed quiet. But a little farther on, it started. The snorting, the grunting, the chortling…Rosa's eyes opened wide in shock.

"That's me?"

Lizzy nodded with satisfaction.

"I had absolutely no idea. I am so incredibly embarrassed!"

Lizzy's smile faltered slightly. Rosa really had no clue that she snored, none at all! Starting to feel a little sorry for the anguished-looking Rosa, Lizzy moved to turn off the evidence.

"Wait a minute," Rosa held up a hand. "What was that?"

"What?"

"Turn up the sound."

Curious, Lizzy punched the volume. Rosa's snoring poured through the speakers loud and clear, but another sound echoed in the background. Both girls leaned in close to listen. Their eyes met in horror!

"H-how is th-that possible?" whispered Lizzy. "You were alone in the room; I locked the door."

From the tape recorder a low gravely voice quivered, sounding inhuman, eerily harsh and hurtful. "...I'm watching you, Rosa...I'm watching you, Lizzy...while you study...while you sleep...I'm watching you...and soon you'll be joining me...forever..."

FOOTPRINTS IN THE SNOW

In the early days of Ontonagon County, a bustling boarding house once stood alongside Old Greenland Road between the villages of Greenland and Ontonagon. The sturdy and spacious establishment provided hearty meals and warm beds to weary travelers, and also the occasional friendly game of cards to those feeling lucky.

One frigidly cold and snowy winter evening a traveling salesman by the name of Mr. John Stonehouse decided he'd better hole up for the night and stopped in at the boarding house. He stepped into the cozy front room, unstrapped his heavy snowshoes, and propped them up against the wall where the packed snow slowly began to melt, dripping into a puddle on the floor. As he signed in at the front desk, he shook out his thick, black overcoat and hung it by the fireplace to hopefully dry out by morning. Not really interested in retiring to bed just yet, he ambled into the sitting room with a mug of hot cider, and soon joined in on an action-packed game of poker.

Now, Mr. Stonehouse is usually quite the talkative type, as one would have to be in the salesman business, and his fellow poker players noticed this about him right away. But when Mr. Stonehouse turned over a particularly excellent hand, four kings to be exact, he excited himself into utter silence for fear he would give away his secret. The other poker players noticed this right away, also, and suspected Mr. Stonehouse of having a winning hand. And not being the types of poker players to let this kind of information go without using it, they all immediately folded or in other words, quit that hand of cards.

Normally Mr. Stonehouse, an even-tempered type of fellow, would have shrugged and then shuffled and dealt a new game, but that week had been a particularly difficult one for him. No one had been interested in purchasing his brand new products, and his family desperately needed new shoes. He had started counting on the few dollars he would win from his excellent hand of cards. When the others folded, Mr. Stonehouse's temper flared as bright as the hot flames singing in the fireplace. He leapt up from his chair, knocking it over backwards, and shouted accusations of cheating to everyone around him. A big brawl soon broke out, with fists a' flying and insults assaulting. Somewhere in the pandemonium, a gun emerged and fired with an earsplitting explosion! Mr. Stonehouse dropped to the floor, dead.

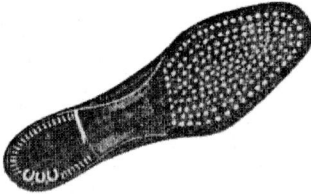

Of course the sheriff arrived the next morning, but by then every one of the poker players, except the body of the deceased Mr. John Stonehouse, had left. So with no suspects still in attendance, no arrests concurred. Time passed on.

The boarding house still stands today on Old Greenland Road, between the villages of Greenland and Ontonagon. The house is a little older and a little shabbier, and a little emptier. An elderly couple by the name of Mr. and Mrs. See own it, and as they didn't need all of that space, and they definitely didn't want to heat the extra floors and rooms, they boarded over the unused portions of the house.

One crispy winter evening, the type where the stars burn bright in the clear, cold sky and the air stands so still one can hear the snow crackling underfoot, Mr. See sat cozily in the sitting

room all alone as Mrs. See had gone to visit a great niece expecting her first baby. Well, actually, he wasn't totally alone, as their large black and white cat named Badger purred contentedly on his lap and their loveable mutt named Red rested his head on Mr. See's slippered feet.

Mr. See had begun drifting into sleep when a muffled knocking jerked him awake. He looked around in confusion, until he realized that someone was knocking on one of the boarded over doors on the other side of the house.

"You have to go around!" offered Mr. See loudly. "That door's boarded over!"

"Woof!" Red added helpfully.

They waited expectantly for a moment, and then the knocking echoed through the empty rooms again, this time more insistently.

"Go around!" Mr. See yelled, a bit impatiently. He didn't especially enjoy unexpected visitors, and besides, all of his pals knew to come to the side door.

Again they waited, but no other sounds emanated from either the front or the side doors. Badger, having been disturbed enough, got up to find a quieter sleeping spot. Mr. See and Red exchanged a confused glance, and then both hauled to their feet with creaking joints. Mr. See peeked out the window, but saw no shadows of movement across the starlit, snow-covered yard. He shrugged.

"Must be them neighbor kids out playing their jokes," he mumbled. "Come on, Red, let's hit the hay." He locked the door, and then he and Red ambled off to bed.

The next morning dawned clear and cold, so Mr. See bundled into his heavy winter coat to take his daily walk with Red. As he opened the side door, he noticed something very curious indeed. He slowly exhaled, his breath blowing out in a frozen cloud.

Fresh snowshoe tracks led around the house and up to the door. And then ended. No one stood waiting on the porch, and no tracks led away from the house.

"That's very strange," he muttered to Red who snuffled intently at the new tracks. "How is that possible, Red? Everyone knows that you can't backtrack in snowshoes, not without leaving a mess in the snow, and yet, where did the visitor go?"

Mr. See pondered the puzzle for a few minutes, until Red pawed at his leg, anxious for his walk. They carefully stepped around the tracks and set out for their morning exercise. At the road, Mr. See paused and looked behind him, eyeing their fresh tracks running beside the mysterious ones. He shook his head in wonder, and then they turned onto the trail paralleling the road through the woods.

About twenty minutes later, Red paused in his mouse hunt to stare intently back at the road.

"Woof," he woofed, part warning and part curiosity.

"What do you see, my friend?" Mr. See turned to look.

Back on the road stood a dark figure in a thick woolen coat. Mr. See didn't recognize him, but occasionally they did pass a visiting winter tourist on their daily walks. Though this stranger's dress didn't resemble the flashy winter gear today's tourists usually sported.

Mr. See raised a hand in greeting; he was reared to be a polite fellow, after all. But the stranger didn't respond. Mr. See shrugged and they continued on their walk.

Red and Mr. See returned home following the roadway. By then, Mr. See had forgotten all about the silent visitor, but Red hadn't. Red began to whine excitedly as they approached the spot where the visitor had stood. The dog dropped his nose to the snowy ground and thoroughly inspected the area. Mr. See stopped in frozen wonder. There in the fresh, previously unmarked roadway stood a perfect pair of snowshoe tracks. But like the set at the house, they ended abruptly, leaving no clue as to

where their owner had gone. A cold, creepy hand clenched at Mr. See's stomach.

"Um, let's go home, shall we Red?" And the pair returned to their warm house as quickly as their feet could carry them.

When Mrs. See returned home later that night, Mr. See met her at the door and hesitantly reported the strange events. The snowshoe tracks still lay undisturbed in the walkway up to the house. Mrs. See immediately became bouncy with excitement.

"I bet you that the visitor is the ghost of old Mr. John Stonehouse, the traveling salesman!" She filled her husband in on the historical details. "The ladies in my choir group told me about

him, but I thought they were just pulling my leg. Wow, we have our own special ghost!"

Over the following years, the See's continued to encounter the mysterious visitor, but always in a similar way, a glimpse in the distance or an unanswered knock at the door. When the couple moved away, they never saw him again, but they'll always fondly remember their ghostly visitor with the snowshoes.

THIRTEEN GRAVES

There is a little known graveyard outside of Menominee, Michigan where bored teenagers like to visit. Way off the beaten path, it provides a bit of privacy for those looking for some space, and a bit of seclusion for those who prefer not to be found. The graveyard, known by some as Thirteen Graves, also provides a grand opportunity to scare the wits out of visiting friends---and yourself.

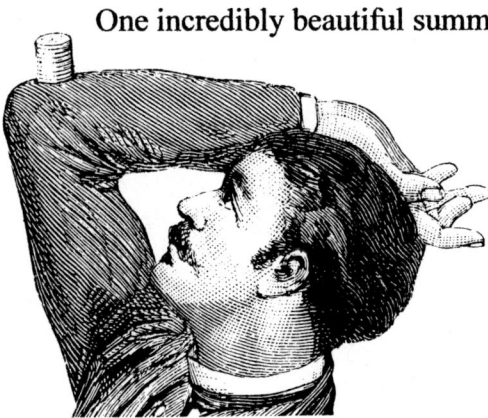

One incredibly beautiful summer day, back in 1974, a fellow by the name of Tim McDowell had his four visiting, out-of-state cousins to entertain. He phoned up a few of his friends, and then set out to meet for a beach party along Lake Michigan. Volleyball, swimming, sun bathing, and a bonfire with roasting hotdogs and marshmallows made for a perfect day. As the sun began to set behind them, the temperatures dropped off and the group gathered close around the fire both for warmth and in hopes the smoke would keep the hungry, swarming mosquitoes at bay.

"Hey, Tim," Nadine yelled across the flames. "Tell your cousins about Thirteen Graves!"

With a little bit of encouragement, Tim consented and began the story. "Years ago, back during the Depression, a family by the name of Millcot lived just outside of Menominee. Poorer than poor, the mother could barely manage to feed her eleven kids. The father never lifted a hand, except to beat on all of them. Dressed in rags and nothing but skin over bones, the kids ran wild while the mother toiled for hours on end in their meager garden,

and then would stand on the street corner begging for people's spare change. She despised begging, but what else could she do with a good-for-nothing husband and eleven hungry kids?"

Tim paused, shaking his head dramatically to earn a few sympathetic, tear-filled gazes from the girls in the group. Shelly snuggled up next to him, placing her head on his shoulder.

"Just as the long winter started to hand the reins over to spring, the family ran out of food. With only a few precious pennies left in the cracked jar on the kitchen counter, the mother decided to walk into town to buy some old potatoes. She could make a watery soup that would at least warm the kids up and fill their bellies for a little time anyway. But when she went to the money jar on the counter, it stood empty. Just then, the father stumbled into the house, drunk on the family's last pennies. The usually submissive mother exploded in anger at the father, yelling that he was killing them all! The father exploded in return, his drunken rage blasting out of control! He killed his wife and then every single one of his kids. He lay in the mess consuming the last of his alcohol, and dropping off into unconsciousness from which he never awoke. The sheriff found them, and the village buried them at the old cemetery, all thirteen of them in a row."

Tim scanned the fire-lit faces of his friends and cousins, all wide-eyed and entranced, even the ones who had heard the story a hundred times.

"They say that there is a curse set on those graves. Anyone brave enough, or foolish enough, to try it will be faced with certain bad luck and maybe even death."

"Try what?" Tim's youngest cousin asked.

Tim shook his head. "I shouldn't tell you; I would hate to be responsible for what could result."

A chorus of objections circled the fire, begging Tim to finish the story.

"Okay, okay, but I warned you. They say that if a person dares to disrespect the graves by first walking across all thirteen, and then stopping at the father's and spitting on his headstone, he or she will be cursed for all time."

The group sat in eerie silence for a moment, only the sound of the fire popping and resettling, and the annoying whine of the mosquito filled the night air. One by one, the teens glanced at each other.

"Let's go try it!"

Three cars caravanned through the village and out into the countryside, where the mostly forgotten cemetery laid unkempt and falling apart. Thick, dark clouds had rolled in, shrouding the stars and moon and any light they may have

offered. The three drivers all left their headlights on, sending six bright beams of light across the overgrown field. The group walked cautiously into the cemetery, stepping amongst the toppled headstones too faded to read and decomposing wooden crosses that marked a life long gone. Tim led the way, walking to the far side nestled up against the edge of the forest. Behind him, a couple of girls whispered softly to each other before erupting into a fit of giggles; his cousins elbowed and wrestled, trying to trip each other over the headstones. Someone let out a loud, reverberating fart immediately followed by a bellowing of protests and laughter.

Tim came to a halt and pointed. "Here they are."

The group stared in silence at the line of thirteen graves, each marked by a simple headstone, so eroded and faded as to be unreadable.

"How do we know these graves belong to the family you told us about?" Tim's youngest cousin asked. "They could belong to anyone."

"You could dare the curse and find out," Shelly suggested. "If you get cursed with bad luck, then you'll know for sure."

"And what happens if there is no such thing as the curse?" his older cousin asked sarcastically.

"You don't believe the story, do you," Nadine accused.

"Of course not; it's just some dumb ghost story used to scare kids straight."

"Then prove you don't believe; dare the curse!"

"Yeah, dare the curse! Do it!"

Shaking his head, Tim's older cousin positioned himself at the far end, raised a foot over the graves and then eyed the crowd.

"Um, maybe you shouldn't," Tim advised. "I mean, why risk it."

His cousin shook his head and slowly stepped down on the graves. He took each
step with significance,
feigning looks of fear
and foreboding to
earn a few nervous
laughs from the
group. At the other
end, he turned, hocked up a big wad of spit and deposited it on the headstone.

Looking around, he turned back to the group and smiled. "See, nothing. No bolt of lightening, no earth opening up to swallow me whole, no strange body odors suddenly emerging—"

"Not now, anyway," Shelly interrupted.

"Come on, let's get out of here," Tim commanded. The whole thing was beginning to make him suddenly nervous. Besides, they were late for curfew already.

Everyone piled back into the cars, with Tim's older cousin offering to drive them back to Tim's house. The convoy pulled back onto the road, single file, with Tim's car bringing up the rear.

That's when it happened. Sure, they were going a little fast, but that doesn't explain why the first two cars past over the creek bridge just fine and Tim's didn't. Did they hit a patch of oil, or did Tim's cousin swerve to miss a porcupine? The car jerked to one side, totally out of control and slammed driver side, into a tree. Four of them managed to crawl out of the wreck. Tim's older cousin did not. He now has to spend the rest of his life in a wheel chair, unable to walk, unable to speak. Some blame it on plain bad luck. Tim and his friends know differently.

WOLF MOUNTAIN

Cole speared another hotdog with his roasting stick and plunged it into the red and gold flames dancing within the circle of stones. All around him, the darkness continued creeping closer, kept at bay only by the cheerful warmth of the campfire and the familiar voices of the guys insulting each other.

"Good gravy, Skunk!" Jerry frantically fanned his hand in front of his face. "Just how many baked beans have you eaten? If you keep that up, you'll gas us out of our tent tonight."

"I didn't have any." Skunk defended himself.

Cole snorted. "That's just the way he smells. How else do you think he earned his nickname? Kids started calling him Skunk five years ago, way back in kindergarten."

Eddie, Cole's older brother and friend to Jerry, tossed another log on the fire, sending up a shower of sparks. "That doesn't seem very nice."

"Oh, Skunk likes it," Cole assured him, turning to Skunk for his enthusiastic nod. "It's his trademark."

"So, let me get this straight; you're known in school for your, uh, unique odor and its concurring nickname. And this pleases you?"

Skunk and Cole nodded at Eddie's disbelief.

"You're one weird kid," Jerry muttered, shaking his head.

"Maybe," Skunk remarked, "but I bet you'll never forget me."

"You do have a point." Jerry reached for the bag of marshmallows. "So, who's ready for some ghost stories?"

"I am!" Skunk reached over and grabbed a handful of the marshmallows, stuffing his mouth without even taking the time to toast them.

"Sure," Cole murmured a weak agreement as his nerves clenched in dread. Spooky stories weren't his favorite kind, as they tended to actually and truly scare him. But he wasn't about to let his friend or big brother know that.

"Eddie, you go first," Jerry directed. "Tell them the one about Wolf Mountain."

"Wolf Mountain?" Cole asked, glad to be distracted for a moment. "Isn't that near here?"

"That *is* here," Eddie grinned at him. "Wolf Mountain is one of the best places to camp in the U.P. I wouldn't take my little brother anywhere less than the best for our first guys' night out together, now would I."

"And it's haunted," Jerry informed them in a creepy sing/song voice.

Cole's short-lived relief at the distraction dissolved like the first snowflakes of the season falling on warm ground. "H-h-haunted?"

"Yup." Jerry stood up and walked over to the tent where he started digging though his pack for something.

"Cool!" Skunk scooted to the edge of his log in anticipation.

Cole pulled his jacket closer, suddenly feeling very exposed in their isolated camping spot, two miles of a hike from their car. His brain scrambled for an excuse, any excuse, to derail his brother's story-telling direction.

"You may have wondered how Wolf Mountain got its name," Eddie began.

Too late.

Eddie continued on in a low, melodious voice. "There are a few stories floating around out there that claim to tell the origins of the name for this particular spot of paradise, but there's only one real story, and I'm here to pass on that knowledge so that it won't be tragically lost through the passage of time."

"Yeah, yeah," Skunk interrupted, "let's get on with it,"

"Patience, young Skunk," Eddie winked at his little brother to let him know he was just joking, "or I'll be forced to feed you to the blood-hungry mosquitoes."

Skunk quickly fell silent.

"Currently, the beautiful wolf lives wild, free and protected here in the Upper Peninsula. But historically, a wolf's life came at a great price; the government actually *paid* people to kill these shy and amazing creatures. Their populations plummeted, as hunters traded wolf skins in for money until the wolf disappeared, dropping off into extinction from almost the entire continental United States!"

Cole shuddered. This *was* a horror story!

"This wolf bounty started in the state of Michigan in 1838 and continued all the way until 1960. In 1965, Michigan placed the wolf under state protection, with federal protection arriving in 1973 with the Endangered Species Act. Finally, wolves are once again a healthy part of the U.P.'s natural ecosystem. As of the year 2004, Michigan has about 360 wolves, with 19 more on Isle Royal.

"Now that you have a bit of background info, I'll continue on with our story. It begins sometime during the late 1800's, when just a few wolves had still managed to avoid the traps and guns of the bounty hunter. A local family by the name of Braymer took a weekend camping trip up on this very mountain. After setting up

camp, the father and older kids set off to hunt down a supply of firewood, while the younger kids slept and played in the shade of their mother's skirts as she peacefully pieced together a quilt. That

left six-year-old Jack, bored and restless, and no one to play with. His mother suggested he go in search of some thimbleberries. If he should find enough, she'd bake a pie when they returned home. Always eager for one of his mother's famous thimbleberry pies, Jack grabbed a bucket and set off on a hunt of his own.

"As luck would have it, that weekend happened to be peek thimbleberry season. Jack discovered bush after loaded bush, and filled both his bucket and his stomach to overflowing. Sticky, slightly sick and very tired, Jack decided to return to camp. The sun had started to drop, sending out long, dark shadows across the forest floor. Jack walked a few steps, but then stopped. He looked around and found nothing familiar, yet at the same time everything looked the same. He'd gotten himself good and lost."

"What an idiot," Skunk interrupted. "Everyone knows you should carry a compass and keep your wits about you when walking through the woods."

"Shh," Cole whispered, entranced in the story despite his nerves. "The kid's only six. I'm sure you didn't know how to use a compass when you were six."

"Meanwhile," Eddie continued, "back at camp, Jack's family had started to worry. The older kids and the father all grabbed torches and then spread out to search the forest. When morning arrived and they hadn't even spotted a single clue, they sent for reinforcements. Every neighbor within fifteen miles arrived to help with the search. But after two weeks of not even finding a single clue, most people began to trickle back to their own homes and responsibilities, believing Jack to be long gone and most likely dead; no way could a six-year-old survive on his own, especially with the temperatures dropping below freezing most every night.

"And it's true, Jack couldn't have survived on his own, but Jack *wasn't* on his own. Sometime during the second night, as Jack curled up into a tight ball beneath a hollowed log, a curious visitor approached. A wolf! This wolf, a lone female, had outlived all of her pack mates who had died at the hands of hunters. Even her spring litter of pups had been killed, and she suffered loneliness and heartache. She cautiously approached the hollowed log, her nose sniffing the strange odor and her ears on constant guard. The moonlight reflected off of her pure white coat as she slipped through the shadows to inspect the suspicious creature. She sensed the immanent danger of humans, yet her maternal instincts compelled her forward towards the obvious

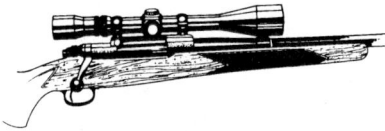

distress noises Jack uttered in his sleep. Her loneliness and hunger for her pack mates, any pack mate, won out and she curled protectively around the sleeping Jack. The two comforted each other throughout the night.

"As dawn broke the next day, Jack woke to find his new friend. Surprised and frightened at first, Jack quickly came to trust the white wolf, so like the white dog at his neighbor's house. Through the following days, she kept him warm and brought food for him to eat, and he rubbed her belly and became a substitute for her lost pack. But she knew he didn't belong with her, and at the first sign of a human, she regretfully sought the stranger out to return the boy.

"The white wolf left Jack in a clearing and circled around to inspect the human. Almost immediately, her keen nose caught a whiff of gunpowder, and her hackles rose in defense. She raced back to hide Jack, to save him from the guns that had killed her other family, but it was too late.

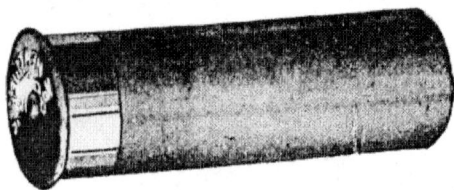

"'I see you,' the hunter whispered under his breath. 'I see you, and your wolf pelt is gonna bring me some money.' But the hunter hadn't seen the white wolf; he had spotted Jack sleeping in the tall grass and had mistaken him for a wolf. He aimed down the long barrel of his rifle and slowly squeezed the trigger…BANG!

"The white wolf leapt in front of the sleeping Jack, catching the bullet in her heart. She dropped to the ground, the red blood staining her beautiful white coat. Jack woke just in time to see his dear friend die for him. Overcome with grief and terror, Jack huddled unseen in the grasses until the enemy claimed the wolf's body and left.

"At first, Jack felt totally alone again, but he soon felt a presence nearby, and he glanced up to see his friend, the white wolf. Not the physical part though; that was gone. But her spirit, a bright and glowing echo of her former self stood before him, just

as beautiful and just as dear. He followed her as she led him through the woods, back to his human family. As Jack received smothering hugs from his parents and siblings, he took a last look over his shoulder at the ghost wolf who said goodbye with a wag of her white tail and a soulful howl into the wind."

Eddie paused for a moment, letting his ghost tale settle in, and then continued. "The white ghost wolf still wonders these forests today and many have witnessed her, especially young boys and girls who have stepped away from their families for a moment. I've seen her; maybe you will too."

A deep, growling wolf howl filled the campsite, causing Skunk and Cole to leap up from the logs with hearts pounding in fear. But the effect was soon lost as Jerry fell through the bushes, holding his side with laughter.

"You two should have seen your faces," he roared, and then he attempted another wolf howl but couldn't quite complete it due to choking on his own mirth.

"That was pretty awesome," Skunk snorted. "Man, I almost peed my pants."

"You okay, Cole?" Eddie asked his little brother. "We didn't scare you too bad, did we?"

Cole shook his head. He hesitated, and then had to ask, "But the ghost wolf, is it true? Does she still roam this forest?"

"You better believe it, kid. I *have* seen her myself, that wasn't just part of the story."

The guys banked the fire for the night and prepared for bed. As they ducked into the tent, Cole realized that he desperately needed to find a friendly tree. Still shaking from the aftereffects of

Jerry's fake howl, he hated to slip out of the camp's clearing by himself, but he wasn't about to admit that to anyone. He grabbed a flashlight and gave in to the call of nature.

As he crept away from the campsite, nighttime noises swarmed his senses. The wind whistled through the branches, tree frogs serenaded each other, an owl called to her mate. Cole jumped as he stepped on a dry limb that broke with the seemingly loud crack of lightning. He forced himself to laugh at his sensitive nerves and quickly located a suitable tree for his business. As he finished, he realized he'd wondered far enough away to not hear the voices of his friend and brother. Cole aimed back in what he though was the most direct path and hurried through the dark woods.

But just as he began to take a step, a flash of white forced him back so hard that he landed on his rear. Shocked, he peered into the darkness trying to make out what had held him back. A white, glimmering shape materialized, and a proud, beautiful ghost of a wolf stood before him.

She waved the fluff of her tail in farewell, and then bounded away.

Cole turned on his flashlight and pointed it at the path. But there was no path! The earth dropped away into a deep crevasse that surely would have killed him had he fallen! Shaking with nerves and awe, he stumbled back into the campsite. His brother stood near the banked fire waiting for him. Not far off the howl of a wolf echoed softly into the clearing. Cole met his brother's eyes and they both knew that they'd heard the call of the ghost wolf.

SAMMY'S STORY

In the early hours of a cold January night in 1960, little Sammy sat by the fogged-over window in the boy's dormitory of the Marquette Orphanage. The ten-year-old couldn't sleep for the nightmares plaguing his mind. But unlike most nightmares, Sammy's wouldn't disappear with the morning sun. His bad dreams originated from the real thing --- that big bully of a kid named Kip. Only a year older than Sammy, but seventy-five pounds heavier and a million times meaner, Kip ruled the younger grades at the orphanage. But his favorite target by far was

Sammy. Anything could and did happen, from the childish pranks of disgusting swirlies and salt in the sugar bowl, to the emotional abuse of heart-breaking insults and insinuating lies, to the more physically threatening gestures of bruising arm punches and deliberate trips down the cement steps. Kip truly made Sammy's already bleak life into a living hell. Sammy had tried complaining to the teachers, but the sneaky Kip always skillfully disguised his ambushes, so the teachers didn't take Sammy's complaints seriously. And when Kip heard about being turned in, Sammy seriously wished he'd kept his mouth shut and had a painful reminder to never try that again.

Sammy sighed, carefully easing his bruised cheekbone against the cold window pane. For the hundredth time, he dug deep for a solution, anything to stop the torture Kip seemed determined to dole out so unequally in Sammy's favor. He'd already tried the adult route, which had failed miserably. He'd tried rallying the younger grades together to stand up to Kip as one overwhelming force. But every one of the kids, minus his best friend Dave, had one hundred percent declined. Not that Sammy blamed them. Why should they risk the wrath of Kip when he already focused it on someone other than themselves --- in other words Sammy, himself.

Deep in the depths of his despair, that other idea, the bad one, crept back into his mind. The weather certainly would cooperate this frigid January. And it had worked for Brian Thomas. *No!* Sammy pushed the unacceptable plan away. Death on purpose never solved a single thing. Besides, Brian hadn't done it on purpose.

About fifteen years ago, Brian Thomas had snuck outside to play in the first snow storm of the season. The teachers locked the doors for the night, not knowing Brian still scurried around in the snow drifts building up a supply of snowballs to launch at the sixth grade girls the next day. Brian came down with pneumonia and died four days later. The older kids tried and sometimes succeeded in scaring the younger ones with tales of Brian's ghost haunting the orphanage.

But Sammy knew life was a gift and not one to be thrown away, especially over a complete jerk like Kip. He would not deliberately sneak out to try and catch pneumonia. It wasn't the answer. He signed again and moved his cheek over a few inches to

find a fresh cool spot. He'd figure out something, and hopefully before he ended up an ugly pile of purple pulp.

Then a strange squeaking noise caught Sammy's attention, sounding a bit like a finger writing on a window's condensation. He sat up and looked around, yet the entire younger boy's dormitory slept soundly with muffled snores and an occasional *frrt* of gas.

The strange noise came again, drawing Sammy's eyes back to the frosted window where two vertical lines had been drawn. Sammy's mouth dropped open in surprise as right him front of him a new line appeared connecting the previous ones...with no visible means of origins. But...how? Despite knowing he sat on the third floor and there being no possible way of someone writing on the outside of the window, he peered through the glass for the culprit. Only darkness and swiftly falling snowflakes met his questioning eyes. He pulled back in time to see three more lines magically appear on the window.

HI

Sammy jumped back from the mysterious message, heart pounding in fear. Without a backward glance he leapt into his bed and pulled the covers up over his head. Trembling in the stuffy and scratchy darkness, he eagerly, and sleeplessly, waited for morning.

All throughout the next day, Sammy could hardly pay any attention in his classes. Who, or what, had written that greeting in the window's condensation? About halfway through math class, an idea hit him, an idea so shocking that it could only be the truth. The ghost of Brian Thomas had contacted him from the dead! Sammy could hardly wait until the wee hours to test out his theory.

The clock chimed two A.M. before Sammy dared return to the window. He fidgeted and paced, waiting for some sort of sign. Then, feeling a bit foolish, he called out in a tentative whisper, "Hello?"

A tense moment passed, and then letters began forming in the condensation.

HI

Sammy blew out his held breath and gulped in some fresh air. Clearing his throat, he asked. "Are you Brian?"

YES, AND YOU ARE SAMMY

The fear slowly drained from him, replaced by hesitant excitement. "Why are you talking to me?"

I'VE BEEN WATCHING. KIP IS A REAL JERK

"You're telling me. Got any suggestions?"

I COULD GET RID OF HIM

"Sounds swell. But how?"

I WILL KILL HIM

Sammy chuckled. "Well, it *would* make things a bit easier. But really, what can you do?"

I AM SERIOUS

A shudder of unease rippled down Sammy's spine. He began to suspect he was dealing with someone a bit more dangerous than an innocent child ghost. "Um," Sammy's voice shook and he paused to clear his throat. "Um, are you Brian Thomas, the kid who died a few years back?"

NO

Sammy took an uneasy step back from the window. "Then who—"

IT DOES NOT MATTER. I WILL TAKE CARE OF KIP

"Wait!" Sammy hesitated as fear seized his tongue. He couldn't let this ghost, or whatever it was, kill Kip! But what if he

148

refused the ghost's offer and then the ghost came after him? He had to try something. Taking a deep breath, he forced his reluctant feet a few inches closer to the frosted window. "Listen, I'm okay. Really. I can handle Kip on my own; you don't have to do anything to him."

HE NEEDS TO BE PUNISHED. SOMETHING WILL BE DONE

Sammy's brain raced for a solution. "In-instead of your s-suggestion," he stammered, "how about if you just scare him a bit?"

JUST SCARE HIM

"Yeah," Sammy continued. "That will teach him a lesson; that will be good enough."

IF YOU WISH

Sammy waited for more letters to appear, but felt relief when none did. He slunk back to bed, pulled the covers over his head and curled up into a tight ball of regret.

Panicked yelling and pounding footsteps woke the entire younger boy's dormitory the next morning. The boys poured out into a hallway filled with pandemonium. Teachers and older boys raced down the stairs in a flood of rowdy uneasiness. With a sick feeling in his stomach, Sammy reached out and grabbed the arm of a guy named Andy, the only fellow racing back up the steps.

"What's going on?"

Eager to share the news, Andy stopped long enough to reveal the raging report. "It's Kip. He started acting crazy! Waving his arms around his head and yelling 'go away' but there weren't nothin' there! Then he jumped out of bed yelling like a monster chomped at his heels, ran straight for the window and dove right out! Broke both legs and even an arm. Lucky he didn't break his neck. Doctor's on his way." Andy hurried off to spread the news to the girls' dorm.

Sammy stood frozen as the other boys pushed past him to get a look. Slowly, he returned to the now empty dorm, and crawled back under the covers. An evil chuckle echoed quietly in the dark, dusty corners of the room. Sammy never again got within two feet of another window in that orphanage ever again.

GHOSTS OF INTERSTATE 90 Chicago to Boston   by D. Latham

GHOSTS of the Whitewater Valley by Chuck Grimes

GHOSTS of Interstate 74   by B. Carlson

GHOSTS of the Ohio Lakeshore Counties   by Karen Waltemire

GHOSTS of Interstate 65   by Joanna Foreman

GHOSTS of Interstate 25 by Bruce Carlson

GHOSTS of the Smoky Mountains by Larry Hillhouse

GHOSTS of the Illinois Canal System by David Youngquist

GHOSTS of the Niagara River   by Bruce Carlson

Ghosts of Little Bavaria   by Kishe Wallace

Ghosts of Des Moines County   by Bruce Carlson

Shown above (at 85% of actual size) are the spines of other Quixote Press books of ghost stories.
These are available at the retailer from whom this book was procured, or from our office at 1-800-571-2665 cost is $9.95 + $3.50 S/H.

GHOSTS of Lookout Mountain by Larry Hillhouse

GHOSTS of Interstate 77 by Bruce Carlson

GHOSTS of Interstate 94 by B. Carlson

GHOSTS of MICHIGAN'S U. P. by Chris Shanley-Dillman

GHOSTS of the FOX RIVER VALLEY by D. Latham

GHOSTS ALONG I-35 by B. Carlson

Ghostly Tales of Lake Huron by Roger H. Meyer

Ghost Stories by Kids, for Kids by some really great fifth graders

Ghosts of Door County Wisconsin by Geri Rider

Ghosts of the Ozarks B Carlson

Ghosts of US - 63 by Bruce Carlson

Ghosts of Lake Erie by Jo Lela Pope Kimber

GHOSTS OF DALLAS COUNTY   by Lori Pielak

Ghosts of US - 66   by Michael McCarty & Connie Corcoran Wilson

Ghosts of the Appalachian Trail   by Dr. Tirstan Perry

Ghosts of I- 70   by B. Carlson

Ghosts of the Thousand Islands   by Larry Hillhouse

Ghosts of US - 23 in Michigan   by B. Carlson

Ghosts of Lake Superior   by Enid Cleaves

GHOSTS OF THE IOWA GREAT LAKES   by Bruce Carlson

Ghosts of the Amana Colones   by Lori Erickson

Ghosts of Lee County, Iowa   by Bruce Carlson

The Best of the Mississippi River Ghosts   by Bruce Carlson

Ghosts of Polk County Iowa   by Tom Welch

To Order Copies

Please send me _____ copies of **Ghosts of the Upper Peninsula of Michigan** at $9.95 each plus $3.25 S/H. (Make checks payable to Quixote Press.)

Name _____

Street _____

City _____ State _____ Zip _____

QUIXOTE PRESS
3544 Blakslee Street
Wever IA 52658
1-800-571-2665

To Order Copies

Please send me _____ copies of **Ghosts of the Upper Peninsula of Michigan** at $9.95 each plus $3.25 S/H. (Make checks payable to Quixote Press.)

Name _____

Street _____

City _____ State _____ Zip _____

QUIXOTE PRESS
3544 Blakslee Street
Wever IA 52658
1-800-571-2665